# HOLLY AND HAL MOOSE:™
## OUR Uplifting CHRISTMAS ADVENTURE

ORIGINAL INSPIRATION BY
Maxine Clark

ORIGINAL CONCEPT BY
Jerry Rees

STORY BY
Cassie Wells, David Miller
& Staci Alfermann

ILLUSTRATIONS BY
Out of the Box Creative

© 2008 Build-A-Bear Workshop
1954 Innerbelt Business Center Drive
St. Louis, Missouri 63114

# CHAPTER 1
# A Bad Day Gets Worse

**H**olly Moose was not feeling jolly, not one bit. She was walking home from school, this last day before the Christmas holiday, her booted hooves scuffing in the slushy-snow on the sidewalk. The heady scent of pine was in the air from the fresh cut trees in the Christmas tree lot on the corner, and festive-colored lights were twinkling along the roofline of every building on Main Street, but none of these things lifted Holly's spirits. She looked up and narrowed her eyes. The cause of her unhappiness and constant annoyance was just up ahead, prancing through the snow, her little brother Hal. "Little"? Ha! He was a full year younger than her but a head, plus antlers, taller. A big moose, favoring their very tundra-statuesque dad. Holly was petite, favoring their mother, whose ancestors came from the taiga pine forests up north, and she was thankful for that. There he was, just up ahead, snorting, pawing at the snow, pretending to ready himself for take-off as if he were one of Santa's reindeer.

"You're a moose, you big lug!" she shouted. "M-o-o-s-e!"

But Hal just grinned back at her, then leapt for the sky… and promptly tumbled head over heels into a snow bank. He came up laughing, shaking the snow off of his coat, looking like a crazy moose… a BIG one.

Normally, Holly would just walk down another block, pretending she didn't know him from Adam Antelope but today was an especially bad day.

"You need to watch your brother this afternoon, Holly," her mother had called to her this morning as she'd darted for the school bus, "I won't be home from work until nearly suppertime and you know Dad's out of town until tomorrow."

"But, Mom!" she had wailed, but the bus pulled up and the front door had already shut.

That was when, what should have been, one of the very best days of the year started to go very, very wrong.

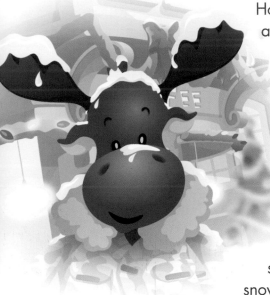

Holly watched Hal running up ahead and found she was feeling more and more sorry for herself. Any other day she would be amused by his antics, but not today. This afternoon was Eliza's holiday *party* and every single moose she knew had been invited and would attend. Holly was Eliza's best friend, so *of course* Holly should be there. She had thought about little else for weeks. Eliza and her father had snow-plowed a maze through the snow drifts in their backyard and there was a small stage under the patio for dancing. And, oh yes, there was going to be a dance contest: the best dance routine to the song *Jingle Bell Rock* would receive a gift certificate to the Moose Mall Emporium. Holly had been practicing her dance for what seemed like forever! Every night, after she finished her homework, she would rehearse in front of the mirror. She hadn't even told Eliza; she wanted her win to come as a surprise.

Ah, well, that dream is over, she thought sadly. Had her mother forgotten about the party? How could she have asked her to watch Hal today of all days? Her mother had smiled at her when she came out of her room this morning.

"You look so nice, honey!" she had said as she bent to kiss her forelock.

Well, of course she did! She had spent an extra half hour getting ready. She had dressed in her best parka with the faux-fur cuffs and collar. She had carefully used her mother's curling iron to add body and wave to her tuft. It was the last day of school before Christmas vacation, it was the day of Eliza's holiday party, Holly looked fabumoose... and all she had to look forward to was watching her little brother.

Big sigh.

"Watch your brother, Holly – the four little words that repeatedly ruin my life," she thought.

She was so lost in thought she didn't even see Hal as he circled behind her and enveloped her in a bear hug, shaking snow from his coat like a furry dog.

"Harold!" which is what she called Hal when she was especially frustrated, "You're getting me all wet!"

But he just laughed, "Holly, Holly! Do you see it?"

Holly looked up, in the direction his gloved hoof was pointing. It was faint but visible: a green glow on the horizon, to the North. Then, as she watched, what looked like green and red flames seemed to swirl up from beyond the edge of the Earth, twist, dive and rise up again. Though she had seen it before, this glorious display astonished her, even in the mood she was in. As she watched, blue and violet joined the swirling red and green.

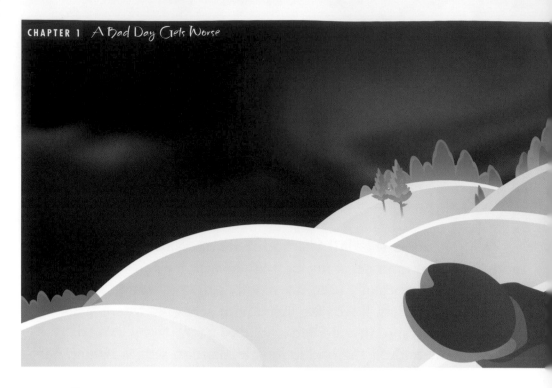

"Holly... I know what that is!"

She turned away from the light show and looked into the eager face of her brother.

"Of course you do. It's the Aurora Borealis, the Northern Lights. We've seen it before and we've learned about it in school. Solar winds interact with the edge of the Earth's magnetic field..."

"No! I mean, I know that's what it is, but it's Christmastime!"

She glared at him, stamping her hoof, "I know that."

But he clung to her arm, jumping up and down, his antlers nearly poking her in the eye, "The Northern Lights only come out in the fall and the spring! This is *winter*!"

Holly looked at him, then back at the dramatic light display on the horizon. "Aurora Borealis is *usually* only visible between September and October or March and April," she said. "That doesn't mean it's *never* visible any other time."

But Hal was so excited he started dancing around her.

"That's the way to the NORTH POLE !"

Holly sighed, one of her deep, exasperated sighs.

"Well, of course it is. Those are the Northern Lights, what other direction would it be in but north, toward the North Pole."

Hal had thrown his backpack on the ground and was pawing through the contents, spilling all of his belongings – books, pencils, paper, an apple and a chewed eraser – onto the damp sidewalk.

"What are you doing? Get up, your knees are getting wet."

He stood up, and handed her a small book, faded with use and age.

"Look at this!" He pointed at a page and she saw a hand-colored drawing of the very same lights. "Just read this part, okay? Please."

She frowned at him, not in the mood to play along, but she read the few lines aloud.

"When the Northern Lights appear within twelve days of Christmas, they are not caused by any of the phenomena we have come to associate with Aurora Borealis, but are the result of the energy emitted from Santa's workshop at the North Pole as the elves rush to finish their toy manufacturing in time for Christmas Eve delivery."

Holly gave her little brother a confused look but read the last bit anyway.

"This is a magic time when wishes are granted and secrets are revealed. Only during this rare occurrence is the road to the North Pole unveiled to the determined seeker."

She looked up and handed him back his little book.

"That's just silly. There's a ton of folklore about those lights."

But Hal didn't want to hear any of that. He just ran ahead, shouting, "Santa's just up there!"

Holly sighed yet again. Then she heard the music. Softly, but distinctly, the rousing chords of her favorite holiday song, Jingle Bell Rock. The sound was coming from Eliza's house, just around the corner. Just a peek at the party, she thought, then I'll head home.

She looked up and saw Hal half a block ahead, on his way toward their house, so she darted around the corner and hid behind the tree in old Mr. Anderson's yard where she could best get a glimpse of Eliza's house without being seen. The party was in full swing. She saw her friends through the front windows, laughing, talking, and dancing. In the backyard, she saw the tips of antlers just above the snow drifts as maze-goers got lost, found their way, and got lost again.

"Oh, they are having such a wonderful time," thought Holly, but she was a responsible girl so she turned around and headed home.

It was at the walkway to her house that she had the first inkling that something was wrong. There was a light covering of snow up the walkway, across the grass and along the driveway... but no hoof prints leading up to the house. The house was dark, the house key was still under the pot on the porch, and there was no sign of Hal.

She turned and looked North. There they were, Hal's familiar hoofprints in the snow, heading up the sidewalk, beyond the paved streets and onto the dirt road, then into the open fields and deep into the snow toward the woods... and straight into the swirling mists of the full-blown Aurora Borealis.

She didn't hesitate: new boots and all, Holly plunged into the snow, following her little brother's tracks.

"Hal!", she cried, but her voice was carried away by the wind. "Hal...", and then she, too, was gone.

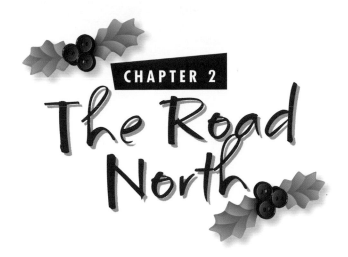

# CHAPTER 2
# The Road North

**T**he blizzard had started an hour ago. It began as a gentle snow flurry, so soft that the flakes seemed to tickle her eyelashes. As she had trudged after her reckless-moose of a brother, she finally had the presence of mind to be delighted at the winter wonderland that spread out endlessly before her.

"I never realized just how beautiful it is out here!" thought Holly. For she was a suburban moose after all and the only tracks she usually made in the snow were along the sidewalk.

She was getting ready to take a picture with her cellphone – one of her favorite things to do, which she would later post to her web site – when the snow started to come down in earnest and she was being battered by the torrential drifts.

"Oh this one will be great," she muttered. Her eyelashes looked like tiny icicles in the picture and they clattered and chimed each time she blinked. Her best parka was soaking wet; her tuft, so carefully curled this morning, was plastered like a drowned rat to her forehead.

For once, Holly didn't care. She'd lost Hal's tracks in the snow and the fear that she had lost all trace of him froze her heart.

"Hal!" she kept calling, but she heard nothing in reply.

The sun disappeared below the horizon; the full moon that was rising to take its place in the sky brought with it a landscape bleached of color. And it got colder, freezing cold. All Holly could think to do was to head toward the swirling Northern lights in the sky. She had to believe that Hal was somewhere up ahead of her doing exactly the same thing on his crazy quest to march straight up to the North Pole.

Then she saw it. Just up ahead. A glow. A campfire? Way out *here*? In the middle of nowhere? The drifts of snow were up to her waist as she made her way toward the orange glow of what had to be flames.

"Eeeeeeeeeeeaaaaaaaaaiiiii," was all she managed to say as the icy ground gave way beneath her feet and she plunged, sliding down into a gigantic ice pit! She hit a big mound of snow with a *whomph*. She flailed at the powdery snow that covered her head and was able to dig herself out quickly.

"Hal!" she cried.

And there he was, grinning at her from ear to ear, "I was wondering when you were going to catch up."

She wacked his antlers so hard that she swore she heard walnuts rattling in his skull. But he kept grinning at her, and she couldn't help but fling her arms around his neck and hug him tight.

"Don't you *ever* do that again!"

"I found the kindling and I rubbed two sticks together. You know, just to help take off a bit of the chill."

First she stared at him, stupefied, then realized what he was talking about.

"You built a campfire on *ice*?"

"I really didn't think about that part."

"Flames *melt* ice, Hal!"

"Cool, huh?" he beamed, "That's how I made this giant ice pit."

"You didn't *make* it, it made itself while you no doubt were not even thinking about the consequences from mixing fire and ice."

He shushed her with a gentle hoof on her arm, "I'm glad you're here. Now you can figure out how we're going to get out."

She sighed and then realized the warmth from the fire did feel nice. She sat down and warmed her mittens over the dancing flames, her no-longer-lost brother beside her, and she found herself smiling in relief. For a moment, in fact, she managed to put it out of her mind that now they were both lost. Hmmm, if she squinted her eyes, she could almost pretend they were camping. If only they had some marshmallows to roast over the open flame, she would almost be content.

Holly looked up and saw a blanket of stars above them. "It stopped snowing."

"Look!" he cried. "The North Star."

And so it was; the star had joined the swirling lights of the Aurora Borealis, like a diamond in an emerald crown. The two rose to their feet, brother and sister stood side by side staring upward.

Then she heard Hal's voice. It was the whisper-voice he used when he said his prayers, the voice he used when he was most sincere. She looked over at him. His arms were raised, his face upturned: he was addressing the North Star.

"Star light, star bright, first star I see tonight. I wish I may, I wish I might, have the wish I wish tonight..." He took a deep breath and whispered, "I wish to lead Santa's sleigh. I wish to fly across the sky with the reindeer to deliver all the presents across the world! I wish I may, I wish with all my might!"

Holly shook her head and muttered sadly to herself. "Dream on, little brother. I wish I could be at Eliza's party but here I am in a snowstorm at the edge of an ice pit in the middle of the wilderness."

Well, she could at least get a picture of Hal, dreaming again, minutes before they would start to freeze...maybe her last picture.

"Hal," she said, forcing herself to be rational and sensible, "We have to get home. Mom will be worried if we miss dinner."

Hal shrugged. "But which way is home?"

Without thinking, she reached out and took his hoof in hers. "I don't know..."

Holly didn't want to tell her little brother that she was out of ideas. Her backpack full of tricks that she could usually rely on... cell phone, laptop...wouldn't help them now. And they definitely didn't cover this on her last school test.

As they stood there wondering what they were going to do, they both began to rub their eyes as something strange came in to view. Were they dreaming? Were they really seeing what they thought they were as the walls of their ice cave began to melt around them?

Hal said, "It's just like I pictured in my dreams." And at that moment Holly knew she wasn't dreaming. She was really taking in the most breathtaking view of the North Pole! The lights down below shimmered on their faces as they stood in amazement. They could make out elves and reindeer bustling through the streets pulling sleds full of toys and goodies.

Hal suddenly shouted, "Come on! Let's go!" His loud boisterous voice shattered the moment…and the ice. It was cracking everywhere!

"What do you mean, let's go? We're on a cliff!" Holly exclaimed.

"But it flattens out at the bottom." Hal shrugged at the suggestion that it might be dangerous.

Holly glared at her brother, "So will *we* if we jump!"

But without another thought, Hal did what he always did. He raised his hooves and bellowed, "Nothing can stop me!" And then with his big moose strength, he threw his sister on his back and leapt over the cliff.

For a moment Hal thought he was flying. The air was all around him, the landscape far below and he felt the peaceful twinkling of stars and time. "This is what it's like," he said to himself, "This is what flying feels like."

"Hal, slow down!" Holly screamed, but it was no use. He was out of control, a rogue moose-toboggan.

"I can't!" he yelled. "Hold on!" Down they went toward the village. He felt every bump, made even heavier with his sister on his back, choking him from holding on so tightly, his ears ringing from her shrieks, and his nose was full of snow and ice.

He started laughing and screamed "Yahoooooo! North Pole here we come!" Even Holly was laughing. Hal was so happy. He thought, "This is the life!"

"Slow down, Hal!"

"Can't! No brakes!" he shouted over his shoulder.

Holly chanced letting go of Hal with one hand and she wiped the snow out of her eyes with her mitten and looked over his shoulder. "Oh, no!" she muttered as they left the hills and went rocketing down the narrow lanes of the village, weaving from side to side, barely missing the stone walls along the little cottages. She clung tighter and ducked her head down as he pitched his head from side to side, his moose antlers spraying snow like windshield wipers.

CRASH! They hit something! Holly looked back in time to see an elf, yes, an honest to goodness elf, get to his feet and stare at them in surprise.

"Sorry!" called Holly.

Whoosh! They shot through the village at top speed and were airborne as they approached the open field, lit with rows of lights.

"We're *flying!*" cried Hal.

"Watch where you're going!" yelled Holly.

"*Uh-oh!*"

Holly looked up ahead. There was a sleigh dropping down out of the sky, coming in for a landing, with Santa Claus himself at the helm. It was pulled by eight giant reindeer, their muscular legs pawing as if they could get traction in the air!  Santa and the reindeer spotted the headlong-tobogganing moose at the same time. On the ground, an elf was using two flashlights to signal to the sleigh and guide it out of the sky. He, too, saw the moose heading straight for him.

"MOOOOSE!" shouted the elf.

"Heads up!" cried Hal.

"Watch out!" screamed Holly.

But despite a valiant effort, the reindeer couldn't turn in time and neither could Hal.

"BLAM!" was the sound of the two young moose colliding with the reindeer-drawn sleigh.

"PLOP!" was the sound of Santa toppling head-first into a snow drift.

"Oh NOOO," was the sound made by the elf watching the two moose skid by, taking out the entire string of lights on one side of the square.

"Yiiiihaa!" shouted Hal as they careened off the retaining wall and came to a stop right smack against the actual North Pole pole!

Holly lifted up her head and looked at the overturned sleigh. "You've really gone and done it this time, Hal," she muttered.

18

Hal sat up beside her and shook the snow from his antlers, grinning from ear to ear. "That was awesome!" His goggles were steamed up and somewhere in all the commotion Christmas lights had become tangled in his antlers.

The reindeer stood at the front of the overturned sleigh looking perplexed.

"Are you two all right?" asked the little elf nervously.

"**HO-HO-HO!**" Santa laughed at the chaotic scene before him, the sound of this wonderful exclamation echoed through the entire village.

"I'm really sorry about that, Mr. Claus." said Holly

"Call me, Santa, my dear." He smiled at her, his blue eyes twinkling.

**FLASH** No way was Holly going to miss a rare chance to get a picture of the big guy. No one was going to believe these shots.

"Excuse me, Sir, I'm Hal and I'm here to fly with your team." Hal walked up confidently and stuck out his hoof. Never mind that he had a blinking string of Christmas lights entangled in his antlers.

A door swung open to reveal Mrs. Claus, "Well what do we have here? Christmas crashers?!"

"No Ma'am, I'm Holly Moose and this is my brother Hal...we're...uh, just a little lost."

"Well the more the merrier this time of year. Welcome. We need all the help we can get. It's almost Christmas and the elves in the weather center are predicting the most terrible storm of the century....I fear Christmas may be cancelled!"

It was these last words that echoed supernaturally throughout the valley. The elves stopped singing, the bells stopped jingling, and the reindeer stopped in their tracks. All of the North Pole seemed to be holding its collective breath.

"Let's get you inside and dried out."

# CHAPTER 3
# Getting Ready for Christmas

"Are you warming up a bit?"

Holly knocked her hoofs together to see if they were still frozen stiff. They made a pleasant *thunk*, like two wood blocks: back to normal. She grinned at Mrs. C. "Almost completely defrosted."

Santa turned to Hal then lifted one bushy white eyebrow. "You're not quite like any reindeer I've ever seen, young man."

"He's a MOOSE, dear," laughed Mrs. C. "Put on your glasses."

Santa reached into his shirt pocket, pulled out his specs, polished them on his shirttail, and looped the wire stems over his ears. He peered at Hal and chuckled. "A moose... so he is. And a very festive one at that."

Sol, the elf, stood up on his chair and clapped his hands together. He had quite recovered from the mishap with the sleigh and he was back to his normal, as Holly would soon find out, officious self. "Enough lollygagging! 'Tis the season! It's almost upon us... we have much left to do!"

"But they're moose, Sol," Santa pointed out.

22

"They'll have to do!"

Mrs. C grabbed her clipboard and was definitely in command. "Holly, you are with me. Hal, the reindeer are already training in the flight simulation building. Meet them there."

"Great, I'm off!" he exclaimed, as he bolted out the door.

Holly straightened her hair bow and looked at Mrs. C. She fidgeted nervously as she stood in front of her. "I'm ready," Holly said timidly.

"Well, dear, what can you do?" Mrs. C asked.

"I thought I could work in the toy workshops. I'm good at fixing things."

"Excellent! Let's go there now. There are only two days until Christmas and we must hurry." Mrs. C turned and walked out of the room. Holly quickly followed.

When they arrived at the workshop, two teddy bear sentries as tall as telephone poles guarded the entrance. She heard the merry voices of the elves, singing while they worked. Could it be? Yes, it was: *Jingle Bell Rock.* With a surge of Christmas spirit, Holly danced a few steps in the snow, delighting Mrs. C with her moves.

"No **TIME**!" cried Sol, a party-pooper if there ever was one.

On the outside, the workshop was breathtakingly magical, but inside there was chaos. As they entered the big room Holly stopped in amazement. "This was where it all happens," she thought to herself. Boxes were stacked to the ceiling. Elves were here from every corner of the world. Sol climbed down the ladder, which stood in front of a large chalkboard containing all of the requests for toys.

"Holly here can help out wherever you need her. We have to finish the toys, just in case Santa can fly." With that she patted Holly on the shoulder, turned and left the workshop.

Holly looked at Sol. Sol looked at Holly.

He eyed the moose looming before him. She was obviously too big to go where elves would fit....how could she help? "Do you think you could..." A screeching, grinding and thumping sound interrupted his words. The big gears running the lines had broken down again. "Well, just try to make yourself useful," he said and quickly left to fix the problem.

Just then someone shouted, "Look out!" Elves were running down the aisle being chased by a toy robot that had gone out-of-control. It raced behind them, knocking down boxes and upsetting carts, saying over

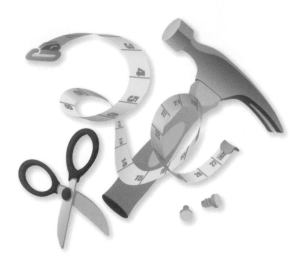

and over, "Nothing can stop me!"

"Reminds me of my brother," Holly laughed. As it passed by, she easily picked it up and turned it off.

Sol came over to Holly. "Just throw that in the recycling bin. It has been nothing but trouble."

"He deserves a good home. I could fix him, it's probably just a little bug in the software," Holly said, looking it over.

"Software, programming, texting, World Wide Web – so many things to keep up on. Tell you what…if you can fix it, you can keep it. I don't have time to deal with him anymore." Sol said.

"Back to work everyone. Oh, and Holly, can you run this over to Santa's house? Mrs. C's chief chef elf said these need to be delivered right away!" He handed her a basket full of delicious smelling muffins with a note from Mrs. C and hurried off to his next task.

Before she left, she noticed some toy moose headed down the assembly line. She pick one up and removed its antlers, attaching them to the top of her little robot friend. "Now you really do remind me of my brother Hal!" she laughed.

Stopping outside the workshop, Holly leafed through the user's manual and found what she was looking for. She tapped the robot's buttons. His eyes flashed and he reset.

The little robot whirred, turned a circle and said, "Thank you, Holly!"

Holly was very pleased. "You're welcome! So you noticed how I saved you from recycling, did you? Oh, it's so nice to be appreciated. I think I'll call you Lil' Hal. Do you like that name? You're like the brother I wish I had." She laughed, smiling at the robot.

Then she programmed more brotherly things for him to say:

"You're a wonderful sister, Holly!"

"I never would have found my dreams without you!"

"I love you, Holly!"

"Thank you, Holly!" the robot said again, buzzed and whirred, and accompanied Holly down the winding path to make their delivery.

## CHAPTER 4
# A Sweet Delivery

**H**olly knocked on the door, then winked at the robot, who still held the basket. "Santa, it's Holly! I've got a surprise for you!"

"Mrs. C sent you this gift." She pointed toward the basket.

Seeing the glazed blueberries popping from the muffin, he beamed, "Oh, thank you, my dear! My favorites! And you too, little one," he added, patting the toy robot's shiny head.

Santa took a delicious bite and glanced at the note from Mrs. C while he chewed. His eyes twinkled. "It's settled. I married the sweetest woman who ever lived."

## Meanwhile, at the Flight Training Center

Hal came running through the barn doors, skidding to a stop. In front of him was a gigantic round wind chamber surrounded by rooftops of all different slopes and slants and styles from around the world. There were rooftops with chimneys and ceramic tiles. There were rocky, thatched and wood-shingled rooftops, and even icy domed igloo roofs!

The reindeer exchanged a few winks and CHUCKLES as they came over to inspect Hal, the newest would-be reindeer. They explained to him that the giant fan of sorts was used to test the reindeer's ability to handle severe weather while flying and landing on rooftops, which was far trickier than anyone might imagine. The big storm predicted for Christmas Eve, was not just any big storm: it was going to be the storm of the century. A storm so big, so fierce, that the sleigh would be almost impossible to fly. The solution? Practice, practice, practice.

It was to be Hal's job to control the level of the wind, or the gusts, from the fan while the reindeer tried to land on the mock-rooftops. Hal would let them have it when they least expected it. He'd pull the lever down and send gale-force winds blasting, knocking them off course, forcing them back into the sky. While the reindeer struggled to get a foothold on the mock-roof, Hal blasted them with a blizzard. He pelted them with hail. Occasionally, one of the reindeer would actually be knocked off course and be sent spinning across the floor. But, within minutes, they were back at it.

"That's it, Hal! Give us what you got! We can't let a storm stop us! Christmas is at stake!"

Then it was time for Hal to take a turn.

Hal put his head down and lifted it up slowly, took two big steps and leapt into the air just like the reindeer. He barely got six inches off the ground. He looked around, embarrassed, and with great determination tried it again. It was the same.

As Hal was sent to the back of the line, his lights were still blinking in his antlers, but now they didn't seem very festive.

Holly and Santa had stopped by to check on the progress. "In all our years we've never seen it this bad." Santa pointed over to the reindeer working in wind tunnel testing area. "Reindeer are great flyers but strong wind is their one big weakness."

They had arrived just in time to witness Hal's faulty flight. Holly could hear some of the reindeer laughing and making jokes about his antlers and how heavy he was. Holly's heart was heavy as she saw her brother struggle, again and again.

FLASH   Holly still wanted to commemorate this moment for those moose back at home who surely would think Hal was crazy when he told the story. Unfortunately with all his jumping around, she only got was his silly face and goofy grin, well at least she would know what had been happening when it was taken.

Santa said, "Looks like he needs some practice or a good set of wings."

Holly went to talk to Hal, now back in control of the wind blaster.

"I can't seem to get off the ground. I'm the only one that doesn't get knocked off the roof in the wind, but I can't seem to take off again." He readied the fan for the next reindeer and then blasted the wind again. The reindeer went tumbling.

He hesitated, "Maybe I can't *fly* with the team. I'm a moose...and everyone says moose don't fly." Hal looked away. "...moose just don't fly..." his voice trailed off.

"A little more wind, Hal," Blitzen said. He turned the fan up to high.

Behind them the storm was getting closer and the real wind was getting stronger. Holly looked at the reindeer and again at her brother. "Those antlers…" she whispered to herself. "The wind swooped perfectly over those moose antlers."

"With a little understanding anyone can fly…" she thought, "Who says moose don't fly?"

Holly and Lil' Hal headed back to the workshop. She pondered Hal's take-off issue and Lil' Hal happily beeped along beside her.

# CHAPTER 5

# Mrs. C Goes High Tech

As soon as Holly stepped into Mrs. C's command center inside the workshop, she immediately saw a problem. While the rest of the North Pole had joined the technological age long ago, Mrs. C's organizational systems could clearly use some modernizing.

Things were done, and run, as they had always been, which left them centuries behind the time. Elves scurried around with heavy ledger books as big as they were, trying to keep track by hand and with quill pens and ink, of all the little boys and girls who were naughty and nice.

Rolls and rolls of parchment paper were what the elves, and Mrs. C, used to keep track of inventory and supplies.

A mammoth chalkboard, hung up near the ceiling, was what they used for the master schedule: every time there was a change to be made, an elf had to roll a ladder over to it, climb up, erase the old numbers and scrawl the new ones. Holly jumped on a ladder and tried to help, but found she did not like this high profile job one bit!

No wonder toy production had fallen a tad behind: it wasn't that the elves weren't working fast enough – they were – it was just that the

way things were organized, it was taking longer to figure out what was going on.

"I know what to do," said Holly, who knew she could help...in her way.

"No, no, no, no," stammered Sol. "We have a tradition to uphold. This has worked for hundreds of years! Nothing must change!"

"You can keep your traditions, but you can also move forward," Holly said and she realized that this might be true of just about everything. She pointed to the toy table where the top toys of the year were laid out. At the front of the line was a teddy bear, right next to it was a mechanical robot. Number one and the runner up.

"How long has the **TEDDY BEAR** been the world's favorite Christmas gift?" she asked.

"More than 100 years thanks to our friend Teddy Roosevelt," Sol answered, picking up the furry friend and looking into its kind eyes. He hugged it tight instinctively and then looked at the robot, realization dawning.

"It takes both," Holly said. "The traditional and the new."

"Can you hand me my backpack, please?"

"Here," he said. "Help us."

Holly opened up her backpack and pulled out her laptop, setting it up on a nearby table and attaching it to the small projector. The screen quickly lit up, startling the elves working nearby. Lil' Hal began typing at robot speed, inputting all the information currently on the handwritten schedule chalkboard.

So while Hal was blowing the reindeer off various rooftops in the barn, his sister not only organized Mrs. C's schedule, but was creating spreadsheets for toy inventory tracking programs, supply analysis programs, and she was able to coordinate all the lists of the good children around the world and print them out according to regions.

She even connected to the elf weather station. The room grew quiet as the looming storm appeared on the large screen. It was coming, that's for sure...she shuddered as she thought about Hal and the reindeer practicing for those high winds.

"It's working!" cried Sol.

Yes, in no time at all, the headquarters of Santa's workshop ROARED into the 21$^{st}$ century, courtesy of young Holly Moose. Almost instantly, production at the workshop speeded up; the Northern Lights were blazing in the sky overhead.

It was only after everything was up and running at lightning pace that Holly felt she could sit down, catch her breath and think about how to help Hal.

# CHAPTER 6

# What Is Time?

"What time is it, Mrs. C?" Holly peered out the two tall double doors but it still looked like dusk.

"Why, it's the same time as when you arrived."

"But... but *hours* have passed! Maybe *days* have passed!"

Mrs. C nodded at the giant grandfather clock at the front of the room. Its pendulum was not moving and its hands were fixed at 4:00.

"I had to stop the clock."

"The clock," echoed Holly.

"Yes, dear. The clock that controls time. How else would we be able to finish all the toys in time for Christmas?" She smiled. "We can't stop time indefinitely, but we can hold it back a little bit."

Holly stared at the clock, her eyelids heavy. "I left school less than an hour and a half ago."

"And your mother won't be worried yet, will she?" Mrs. C gave her

a hug. "That's a blessing!"

"Hmm," Holly thought – it always did seem like it took extra long for Christmas to come every year and now she knew why.

She led Holly outside, where the storm was beginning to brew. "I've had a room made up for you in the house. Why don't you get a little rest?"

But there was too much to do for Holly to sleep now. Christmas needed her.

The storm was bad and getting worse. She bundled her scarf up tight against the wind and looked around for Lil' Hal.

"You would have to be strong as a moose to fight this wind" she thought. "That's why my brother would be great. That's why he shouldn't give up his dream, he was meant to fly with that team!'

At that moment an idea clicked in her mind...springs to help Hal with lift off! She grabbed Lil' Hal and went back to the workshop for supplies. Lil' Hal helped Holly remove the metal runner from a sled and bent them into the shape of springs.

They made their way over to the reindeer barn, hoping to find Hal getting some much needed rest, he'd been practicing so hard!

"Be really, really quiet, okay?" Holly whispered to the little robot and it nodded its little mechanical head.

Holly kneeled down and slipped one of the spring shoes onto Hal's hoof and secured the strap. Hal stirred, deep in his own dream; both Holly and the little robot froze, but Hal settled back into sleep. The little robot handed her the second shoe and she slipped that one on, too. Holly mimed wiping her brow; the little robot did the same.

"That will put a spring in his step," she smiled, "and elevate his dreams again."

"Oh, one more thing before we go," she whispered as she carefully untangled the lights from Hal's antlers.

They tiptoed out of the room and closed the big barn door gently behind them.

"Whew!" said Holly once they were out of earshot, and the little robot nodded.

She and Lil' Hal headed back to the house to rest and recharge before another exciting day. As Holly lay down, Lil' Hal came over to her, put his little flashing head near hers.

"Thank you, Holly." He clicked and whirred. He watched her close her eyes. He reached out his arm and touched hers before he powered down and slept too.

Dream!
Believe!

think... think...
ideas?????

# CHAPTER 8

# Two Moose Who Saved Christmas

**J**ust a short time later, every workshop elf , every citizen and every creature of the North Pole was gathered in the town square, helping load bag after bag after bag of toys into the sleigh. Santa was dressed in his best Christmas wear, his white beard combed and curled, courtesy of Mrs. C.

"They're coming!" someone shouted in the distance and suddenly all the people and all the creatures hurried to line the sides of Main Street. It was like a parade. Santa's reindeer were in full harness, bridles jingling with tiny silver bells. Their hooves were polished, their coats gleamed. Big eyes shined with excitement...or was it nerves?

Mrs. C, who was standing next to Santa, was able to see the worry in his eyes as he looked up at the storm clouds gathering overhead.

"If it's too dangerous, dear, you must turn back."

As if almost on cue, the wind whipped down through streets, nearly toppling the elves waiting to witness the famous flight.

"Cancel Christmas?" he cried, shocked that she would suggest this.

With these words the North Pole was silenced. Not the note of a caroler, nor the giggle of an elf, nor the rustling of last minute wrapping... just the low harsh whistle of the wind as it drove down the mountain.

"Oh my dear, you may be right," Santa said sadly as he considered the safety of his team of reindeer.

Suddenly there was a commotion, it looked like a stray sled had broken loose near the workshop and was plunging down the hillside into the crowd.

The crowd called out together: "Watch out!"

Santa stepped forward and stared at the oncoming sled. On top were Holly Moose and...a little robot Moose, but what were they carrying?

"You're a wonderful sister, Holly" it beeped as it road along on the sled.

"I didn't know you had a little brother," Dasher teased Hal.

The sled skidded to a stop into a pile of snow, and Holly began unloading it. She worked for hours to make Hal's dream invention a reality. Hal ran to help his sister, and the crowd leaned in closer to see what they had on the sled.

"MOOSE antlers?" asked Santa.

"Well, yes sir, but a lot more than that," Hal replied.

Holly handed Santa the drawings and calculations.

"These antlers give your reindeer the extra lift they'll need, just like me, if you get caught on a rooftop during the storm," said Hal.

Santa was about to argue, but then he bent down and studied the calculations. He looked up, his eyes twinkling merrily. "I think it just might work!" He turned to the reindeer. "Come on team, everyone put a pair of these on!"

The inventions slipped right over the reindeers' pointed racks, making them broad and sturdy – as wide as wings and as tight as sails.

Just when Hal thought it couldn't get any better, Santa called out to him, "Hal, I'm going to need you flying with us – with this storm, we'll need all the lift we can get!"

Dasher leapt up for a quick test flight. The storm battled back, but it didn't stop him.

And so it was that each of Santa's eight reindeer became transformed into mighty moose.

Christmas cancelled? Not a chance.

So it came to be that Hal Moose would lead Santa's sleigh on this stormy Christmas Eve. With the lift provided by the sail-like antler coverings, the reindeer would be able to navigate through the wickedest of bad blizzards and maneuver around whatever world-wide weather conditions they might encounter.

The 'rein-moose-deer' were all hitched up with Hal wearing his spring boots in the lead. Santa lifted his voice to call out in the wind "On Dasher, On Dancer, On Prancer...ahem" Santa corrected himself "On Hal, On Dasher, On Dancer...oh let's just go!" and with that the sleigh team and the sleigh began to lift into the sky.

At that very moment, Holly noticed a change. She wasn't sure if others noticed it, but it was very strong in her own heart. The snow didn't seem so cold. The wind didn't seem so strong. Adventures didn't seem so daunting. She felt more comfortable in the world than she had ever felt before, and was very proud to have her brother, Hal, just the way he was.

So when Hal stopped Santa and came up with his craziest idea yet – that Holly should fly around the world beside Hal on the sleigh team on this very special Christmas Eve – she didn't rant about how many miles they would have to fly, or how afraid of heights she was, or how he would probably get them into trouble and she would have to save them, she simply smiled and replied, "Thank you, Hal."

Then together, Holly and Hal each raised a hoof against the wind and shouted, "Nothing can stop us!"

The heavy sleigh groaned and the harnesses strained. The reindeer dipped their mighty shoulders and angled their canvas-covered antlers in preparation for the lift off. Hal bent his knobby moose knees for a terrific spring-loaded launch and suddenly they were airborne, but not quite high enough. Hal flew a tad too low near the decorated street lamps and somehow managed to get another set of Christmas lights tangled in his antlers! But he quickly re-gained height and speed as the North Pole citizens cheered on the festive flight that disappeared into the stormy night bringing toys and goodwill to children everywhere.

# CHAPTER 9

# What Bad Day?

Holly Moose was feeling jolly, from her toes to her tuft. She was walking home from school, this last day before the Christmas holiday, her booted hooves scuffing in the slushy-snow on the sidewalk, grinning from ear to ear.

Just up ahead, running through the snow, was her little brother Hal. He was pretending to ready himself to take-off as if he were one of Santa's reindeer. Suddenly he stopped, looked up, and looked back at her. He ran towards her, nearly knocking her down as he slid to a stop.

"Holly! I had the strangest... daydream!"

"It wasn't a daydream, it happened. I was there, too. Look." Holly pulled her cell phone out of her parka pocket and held it up. There were all her pictures, including her favorite one of all: the team of rein-moose-deer. Then she reached up and unzipped Hal's backpack, pulled out his spring-loaded boots and held them up to show him.

"See? It all happened."

He took the boots, slipped them on and fastened the straps. He smiled as he bounced. "I thought I dreamed it."

"You did. And then it all came true."

"But, Holly, most of it happened *tomorrow*, on Christmas Eve". How could it be *now*?" Hal said as he waved his hoofs around them, at their familiar neighborhood, at the familiar streets.

"As the North Star rose on Christmas Eve, I whispered "Star light, star bright, first star I see tonight…""

"What did you wish *for*?" he asked, bouncing closer.

"Just to return here, to this moment in time. If they can stop time up there at the North Pole, they can certainly turn it back a bit, too."

It was at that moment that they both heard the sounds of Christmas music and laughter from around the corner, at Eliza's house. The *Party* was in full swing.

Hal smiled at her and nodded in the direction of the party. "Ah, I get it… so you wouldn't miss Eliza's party."

"So *we* wouldn't miss it," she said as she smiled and grabbed his arm. "I was hoping you'd be my dance partner in the contest."

"You want ME to go with you to the party?"

"Of course I do." She smiled. "And after that, let's go home. I'm exhausted," she said and she couldn't quite stifle a yawn.

A little voice said, "Thank you, Holly!"

Both moose turned around and looked down at the little robot, devotedly following in their footsteps.

"What are we going to tell mom about the robot?" asked Hal.

"That he deserved a good home." And she reached down, lifted it up, and the three went happily on their way.

# CHAPTER 10

# Christmas Eve

## "Time for bed, kids," said Mom Moose.

"Okay," said Holly as she set up a tea tray near the fireplace.

"We just want to set out Santa's snack," said Hal.

Holly uncovered the basket. In it were three plump blueberry muffins.

"Muffins? But Santa likes milk and cookies," questioned Mom.

"I think he'll like these muffins just fine!" said Holly with a wink at Hal.

"Well, off to bed or Santa might not come."

"Yes he'll be here tonight. We know...he'll be here."

And so it happened that Santa was able to deliver presents and smiles that stormy Christmas Eve thanks to a brother and sister moose who were filled with big ideas and even bigger dreams.

# THE END

DISCOVER MORE holiday FUN at
HAPPYHOLLYBLOG.COM!